Al Katar
Other Books of Fiction

THREE BROKE COMICS

Al Katar

authorHOUSE®

AuthorHouse™
1663 Liberty Drive
Bloomington, IN 47403
www.authorhouse.com
Phone: 1 (800) 839-8640

This is a work of fiction. All of the characters, names, incidents, organizations, and dialogue in this novel are either the products of the author's imagination or are used fictitiously.

Published by AuthorHouse 08/30/2018

ISBN: 978-1-5462-5832-2 (sc)
ISBN: 978-1-5462-5831-5 (e)

Print information available on the last page.

This book is printed on acid-free paper.

Introduction

Three broke comics involved the coming together of the individuals from three different areas of society. That by their circumstances of life come together to accomplish an economic goal of winning a comedian contest.

Follow these three common peoples on their journey to succeed.

Chicago

Chicago the Windy City, Chi-Town sometime referenced to, set on the western shores of Lake Michigan. This historic city is the center of culture and innovation in Middle America. Chicago a magnet to a changing world, that embraces all peoples. Our three heroes are in the right place at the right time. You the reader are invite to follow their rise to the top. So buy a ticket, take a seat and enjoy the ride.

As the sun rises over the great City of Chicago, Illinois, our soon to be heroes awaken to the hustle and bustle of the city, where they live on the south side the suburbs and up town of the city. The first of our three characters is Miss Mary.

Mary is the mother of two young children with a live-in boy friend. She is a praying and singing woman and resides on the south side of the Chicago's rent controlled apartment complexes.

The second character is James a construction worker of a middle class family. He lives in the suburbs of Chicago, with his wife and three kids.

The third character is Rodney a single up and coming advertising executive with many years at his firm. Rodney lives in an upscale condo just off Chicago miracle miles.

All three of our perspective hero's represent

all Americans trying to reach and obtain the American and personal economic dream

Mary awakens to her alarm on her cell phone. She puts on the coffee to have a fresh cup of java. Without it she cannot get her day going. She sings religious hymns and read her bible to give thanks to her God for his blessing in her life.

She wakens the children so they can prepare to go to day care and first grade. Her live-in boyfriend has been unemployed for the last nine months. He seems to not too be able to find any type of job according to him. That would be worthy of his talents.

He seems to think the job has to come and knock on his door to find him. They both argue about the unemployment issue from time to time. But never the less she sends the kids off to school with a kiss, as she prepare her own self for work. As Mary depart out her front door, she sees a late rent due notice placed on her door. The rent control manager for the city Ms. Susan says her rent is pass due and must be paid soon!

Mary works at the city's biggest laundry. To get to work she catches the bus line or receives a car ride with a fellow co-worker in bad weather.

Mary arrive at work with her doo rag on her head. The temperature in the fifty plus year old building is above average, because of all the dryers and they are very noise.

The boss is riding her, asking to pick up the pace as many more trucks arrive with laundry from across the greater Chicago area.

Mary is grateful for her job of five years, but it's taxing her physical endurance. She wants a better job, but the steady pay check is what she needs to support the family at this time.

Mary is staring not to feel well in her head and is deciding to ask her boss can she go home early.

James on the other hand awakens to the smell of coffee and bacon being prepared by his wife of ten years.

After finishing breakfast and putting on his steel toe work boots. He kisses his wife and kids and says I love you as he settles into the seat of his older model pickup truck.

The Chicago rush hour traffic can be quite a challenge as his job is in downtown Chicago, working on building the latest skyscraper of its beautiful sky line.

James arrives on the job sites and goes right to work. During his break he is called over to the office. He is told that his portion on this job will be finished at the end of the week. So he will be laid off until another job can be found.

James tells his boss he needs to work at another job as soon as possible. On his way home James ponders his immediate future. He decides to stop by his favorite automotive store to pick up a few things for his aging pickup truck on credit. Sam the manager is not that all excited to see James, with his overdue account. Sam asked James to help bring his account under control; as he receives more parts. James continue on the road and sees a billboard on the highway that's says Jakes Bar happy hour, two for one drinks. So he decides to drown his sorrows at the next exit for a few minutes at Jakes Bar.

Rodney our third character in this journey awakens by the sound of his hi tech appliances,that automatically turns on his clock alarm, coffeepot, and television. He jumps in the shower to ready himself for the work to be done at his office this day.

Rodney sits down to breakfast as he reads that morning newspaper and watches the price of stocks on the New York stock exchange. Later he leaves his parking garage in his sports car, not far from his downtown office building. He pulls into his private parking space with his name on that space.

Rodney works on the eighteen floor of his office complex. He is greeted by his secretary and handed a list of phone calls to return, along with a note of a board meeting to be held that after noon.

After a great lunch in the company cafeteria, the board meeting starts. As each department head gives their quarterly sales report. Rodney gives his report last. His department sales are even or down compared to his last report in a down economic.

The meeting ends and Rodney boss ask him to stay behind. Rodney is told that his department is to be sold to another company and he is to be laid off as soon as the sale is finalized.

Rodney leaves work later that day disappointed, knowing he has to rebuild his career all over again. So unfocused he misses his exit back home and so doing he sees a sign that says Jakes Bar two for one happy hour drinks. So he decides to drown his sorrows for a while.

Mary still working hard, but is feeling weak, asked her boss to let her go home early. She takes the city bus, which travels over an hour to arrive back at her home, before her two kids come back home from school.

She opens the front door slowly, not to disturb her live-in boyfriend, thinking he's taking a nap. As she approaches the bedroom she hears strange voices from two difference people.

Mary slowly opens the bedroom door and sees her man in bed with another woman, its Ms. Susan the city rent control housing office manager. Both lovers are surprised, as both at the same time try to explain the situation away too no avail.

Mary is very angry and tells the woman to get out as she puts on her clothes. Mary tells Ms. Susan I guess the rent is paid now! Her boyfriend on the other hand is another matter. She settles down and catches her breath and calmly ask him to pack up his few belonging and be gone when she returns.

Mary calls her mother over to her apartment to take charge of her two kids when they arrive home from school.

She leaves the apartment to catch the "A" train to destination unknown, to clear her head of man and future. After an hour of riding, she sees a sign reading Jakes Bar and Grill two for one drinks happy hour.

She thinks why not; let me get lost in my sorrows for a while. Drink my blues away before another day comes.

Now all three of our future heroes are at the same place at the same time, Jakes Bar and Grill. Now the magic, the chemistry can begin that will change their lives and the comedy world.

Jakes Bar

Jakes Bar is a corner stone monument in the city of Chicago. Every town in America has a Jakes Bar. A shrine, temple or a getaway place. Where all your sorrows can temporarily be placed on hold. Where everyone has something their hoping to forget for a while. Everyone is equal and no personal judgment will be given.

That's Jakes Bar come on in for a while.

At Jakes Bar the happy hour is well under way, filled with some of Chicago's best and not so best.

Mary is approached by a few men with bad pickup lines. She politely dismisses them all. She orders two drinks from the bar. As she backs up and turns to find a seat, she bumps into and spills both her drinks on the floor.

The gentleman takes the time to profusely apologize and offers to buy her another drink, she politely refuses. The gentlemen insist, so she gives in graciously.

After she receives her new drinks, they both look for a table on the crowded bar floor.

They find a table with one other person seating there, with two open chairs. They ask for permission to joint him. He says sure I can use the company.

They introduce themselves to each other. Hi my name is James, my name is Mary, and hi my name is Rodney.

As the three of them discuss small talk, the liquor starts to loosen their tongues. They discuss their life problems of the day. With joking and laugher at each one's problem, they order more drinks to mass each other's pain.

After an hour or so of pain removal, they excuse themselves to go to the men and women rest rooms. Rodney and James while washing their hands, notice a contest poster on the rest room wall.

It says comic teams wanted, local, regional and national levels. Five million dollars in contest money to be won by the winners. Two million dollars to the winning team at the national level. Must be a team of no less than three adults. Entry fee is one hundred dollars per person. See web site for more information www.threebrokecomics.com LOL.

Rodney records the contest poster information on his smart phone. As all three returns to their table, James explains to Mary what they saw on the contest poster. Mary says that's the same poster in the women's restroom.

Rodney says I think we three can win the contest. We have good chemistry together; think we proved it here today. James and Mary are very reluctant, making excuses.

Mary says I have two young kids at home and work all week. James says I'm a dedicated family man, when can I find time. Rodney says what do we all have to lose? Rodney is full of confident and explains he once managed a singing group.

They all three people exchange Phone numbers with Rodney insisting on arranging another meeting later that week. All three depart the bar to call it a night and went back to their homes, thinking of the possibility of winning.

Later that week Rodney convinces Mary and James to have a business lunch that Saturday afternoon at a quiet neighbor hood soul food café on the south's side of Chicago.

Rodney arrives first to set the mood or atmosphere. Mary and James are on time together. They all make their menu order. As they await their food.

Rodney hands Mary and James each a three ring binder. Mary says what is this! Rodney says this is our operational or guide to us winning the comedy contest. Inside is a list of do's and do not's, mission statement and a special phone number.

James says what is this cell Phone number all about man. Rodney explains this is for you guys use only. When you call it, leave your name, time and subject matter. The information will be recorded and the voice information will show up on my computer screen in an email voice message. I can hear your routine, give advice and place it in a file, to be edited later.

They all agree to the system. The food arrives and they have a wonderful lunch. They finish their business lunch and each one returning home, knowing what each one has to do.

The next work day at lunch Mary explains to her two closest girlfriends Marilyn and Sally, the opportunity of winning the first stage of the comedy contest, being the local comedian contest.

Marilyn encourages her and wants to buy tickets to the local contest.

Sally on the other hand has the complete opposite view. Sally says she is setting herself up for disappointment and humiliation. Why put yourself through that type of disappointment and public humiliation. Just be content with what you got going for yourself. Think about your family. Mary says I am, as the lunch break is ending.

James is found working on his truck in his garage. His father in- law Joe is visiting from out of town for the week end.

He asks to lend a hand to help fix the truck along with small talk. The discussion finally gets around to James unemployment situation.

Joe says to him if things don't work out in Chicago, his family can move out of the state of Illinois and move in with him. There James could work at his business and maybe operate, manage and own the entire company once he retires. That proposal was well received by James, until his father in-law says, and by the way that comedian contest your wife was explaining to me that you're involved with. That's a losing situation for a guy like you. Don't set yourself up for failure. Joe would not stop talking negative about the contest, until James had enough, he responses!

Joe with all do respect, my unemployment status does not equal failure! This is my one shot in life, where I can be my own boss for the first time in my life. If I fail, I can say I had my shot and not keep looking back over my shoulder. Can you relate to that please sir? A moment of silence occurs. James wife yells out dinner is ready guys.

With two weeks left before the local contest. The three are working hard on their approach and delivery, doing research and encouraging each other.

Finally the day of the big show is here. The three arrive at the night club on the south side of Chicago. The club is packed, standing room only. The team is nervous but confident.

There are other comedians groups from all parts of the state of Illinois and the region.

The judges are at their table. The master of ceremony (MC) takes the microphone and explains the rules. There are twenty groups registered and twenty numbers in the glass bowl.

Whatever numbers the team's representative pull? That will be the number in which your group will take to the stage.

Each member can only be awarded 33.3 points per member. All group points are to be added together to receive the total score. The group with the highest overall score will be the stage one local top winner. Top prize winner 12,000 dollars, and be able to move on to the regional contest in Saint Louis Missouri in one month.

Mary is asked to pull a number for their team. She pulls the number 13, lucky 13.They all say with a laugh.

The bell sounds and the contest starts. The team observes the other teams go up on stage ahead of them.

Some groups are good and some okay. Others are booed off the stage with low scores.

Now its three broke comic's team turn. Rodney feels he has to go on stage first to give his partners courage and confident.

Rodney takes to the stage and grabs the microphone and starts his routine of five minutes; he receives a few good laughs and applause.

Next up for the group is James; he delivers an average performance, but did relate to the crowd.

Now its Mary turn, with knees knocking she almost loses her footing and stubbles to the microphone. The crowd laughs as that was part of the presentation.

Riding that confident boost she starting to deliver a 50- 50, but average performance. She make jokes talking about her family life and work life that relate to the audience.

Mary leaves the stage unsure in her mind of the things she said. Did she help or hurt the group chances of finishing first or second.

The three gather back stage to discuss what

happened on stage. No matter that decision is in the hands of the judges.

As they watch the last of the comedian teams finish their routines, all of the comedian teams are asked to return to the stage, to hear the winning comedian's scores. Of the two groups that will move on to the regional contest in Saint Louis, Missouri.

Three broke comic's team stand together with Mary in the middle holding hands. The first runner up is the group from Champaign, Illinois, with an overall score of 78.

The second runner up is announced and you can hear a pin drop. Its three broke comics from Chicago, Illinois.

The group congratulates each other as if the weight of the world has been lifted off their shoulders. They receive their second place check of $8,000 dollars.

They disband and go home, with a new outlook on life, thinking about the future possibilities.

With one month to go before the regional contest, the team is working hard coming up with new material. Because in a competition, you don't want your competitors to cut your material force down, into the eyes of the judges.

At work Mary buys Marilyn and Sally lunch at the food truck, as she has a little extra money in her pocket. Marilyn is continuing to give encouraging words of support to Mary. While on the other hand, Sally is still on the player hating trip says "yes kid, you got lucky."

That Sunday Mary goes to church with her two children. She sings in the church choir and is assigned to sing a solo. Her two kids are also in the youth choir. As the church service starts, the pastor says today's sermon teaching will be directed on faith. Turn your bibles to James 2:14-26, where it reads faith without works is dead. Mary co-workers Marilyn and Sally are also at church today to hear Gods word.

After the sermon its Mary turn to sing her solo, titled Jesus loves me. After she finishes she moves down out of the choir stand to direct the youth choir to sing a song that they

have been practicing for a month that Mary
wrote, called "My Heart".

The children choir stands up and Mary
direct them

My Heart…My Heart….My Heart…My
Heart
My Heart……. is singing about His love!
Singing about His love!
Bird   singing….fish   singing…Animals
singing
Their singing about His love!
Their singing about His love!
When I wake up in the morning the sun is
shining. The stars are shining.
Their singing about His love!
Their singing about His love!
Their singing about His love!

I go to the forest to pick some flowers
Bees singing, Flowers singing, Butter flies
singing
Their singing about His love!

Their singing about His love!
Their singing about His love!
I go to the mountains to see some snow
Bears walking, foxes walking, Deer's walking
Their singing about His love!
Their singing about His love!
Their singing about His love!

I go to the ocean to see some birds
Birds singing…fish jumping
Their singing about His love!
Their singing about His love!
Their singing about His love!
I went to church to see Gods love!
Children singing….Moms singing…
Fathers singing….Choirs singing
Their singing about His love!
Their singing about His love!
Their singing about His love!

His love is forever!
Amen!

The church audience stands and join in on the second chorus. The church is alive and rocking and end with thunderous applause.

James on the other hand goes to the auto parts store to make a payment on his overdo account. The store manager Sam greets him with skepticism, until James shows him the money. He buys a few other items for his truck and returns home to his family.

He arrives home to find a few extra people at his home. Mostly co-workers and neighbors and their kids. His wife has a few extra dollars from the local win. Has decided to have a surprise back yard barbeque to celebrate. His friends want to encourage him and learn more about the comedy contest going forward.

James is handed a beer to quench his thirst. His friends are looking and treating him as if he's an up and coming super star. The kids are jumping in and out of the above ground kitty pool. James is being sprayed with water from the kids playing with the water hose and water cannons.

As he explain the rules of the contest to his

friends. Suddenly out of the blue a reporter and camera crew shows up in his back yard. To interview him about three broke comic's chances of winning the next stage of the contest in Saint Louis, Missouri.

James is being overwhelmed with questions. He thanks the people for coming out, but wishes the questions would stop 'and the people would go home. As the women shout out loud, dinner is ready come and get it! Finally James thinks to himself, the pressure is off. Can't eat and ask him a question at the same time. With all bellies full and sleepy, even the press everyone goes away satisfied.

Rodney is exploring new ideas of branding and marketing the team overall image through merchandizing and sponsorship. He's even working social media creating various online tools and building a three broke comics.com website.

Later that evening Rodney is to attend a reception given at his girlfriend Traci father's home. It's a charity event to raise money for a new children's wing at the local hospital. A black tie affair to say the least. Rodney arrives at the father's stately mansion with its large green lawns with horse stables in the far corner of the property.

Many of the father's guests have already arrived. The city's well to do, old money as well as new money. A valet parking attendant takes Rodney's car from him to park it. At the top of the stairs he is met by his beautiful girl friend Traci, dressed in a stunting black dress and with a light kiss on her cheek. They walk arm and arm into the main ball room, to where they meet her parents.

They make small talk as to the purpose of the nights gathering. Rodney hands the father an envelope that contain a donation for the hospital building fund. He says thanks as the elder couple move away to attend to the other guest.

Rodney and Traci escape to the baloney to find a quiet place to talk about their future life plans. Rodney get's down on one knee and opens a small box with a large diamond ring and purpose's; and ask for Traci hand in marriage, she excepts. She is so very happy; they kiss to cement their love for one another. Traci rushes downstairs to tell her parents the good news of being a fiancée. The butler rings the dinner bell and says dinner is served. The young couple makes their way to the dining room to be seated for a night of fun, food and drink for a good cause.

Saint Louis

Saint Louis, Missouri the historic city of the mid-west. Saint Louis, the historic gateway to the west. A city blessed by the Mississippi river that cools the soul of the city. Its brown waters filled with rich nutrients that feed the nation. That's why this great city was chosen to cool and feed the soul of our three hero's and the world.

The day of the regional comic contest is here. The team arrives at the Saint Louis convention center. The atmosphere is electric as some of the best wannabe comics in the world come together for this historic showdown. Where the top three teams will move on to the finals in New York City.

Mary has been voted the team good luck charm to pull another stage appearance number from the fish bowl. She pulls the number 5 out of 10 teams. Rodney and James are working the crowd with the team internet business cards and taking selfies with newly won internet fans that traveled to Saint Louis.

The master of ceremony brings the people into order and explains the rules with the prize money to be given. First place 100,000 dollars, second place 75,000 dollars, and third place 50,000 dollars. The rest of you losers 5,000 dollars per team and the bell rings and the contest starts now!

As the team await their turn on stage Mary is approached by a handsome young man in charge of lighting for the contest production company by the name of Tim. Tim makes small talk and says I saw you In Chicago and you where great. Mary is not feeling Tim's rap lines.

She tells herself I have heard it all before. This isn't her first rodeo with men; she has two kids to prove that fact. Tim ask to have dinner with her after the shower, he corrects himself and says show and maybe exchange phone numbers.

Mary does see some possible potential in the young man. She says this is the deal. If my team wins it's a date. It we lose I'll call you from Chicago. Tim accepts the offer; he says it's a bet!

Its three broke comic team turn. Rodney goes first and connects with the crowd. James has the crowd laughing with some new sound bits of famous people and it's a hit with the audience.

Finally its Mary turn to please the judges.

She open up with her new routine; the first joke; why did the chicken cross the street, silence from the crowd. To get too the other side of the road she says. My second joke why did the apple fall from the tree and hit the man in the head; the crowd is dead silence; gravity she says. You could hear a pin drop to the floor.

Rodney and James are in shock at these old school yard play jokes; thinking all is lost. Then Mary says, I see these jokes are not working. Dead silence; even Tim is thinking no date to night.

Mary with her head bowed, suddenly says lets all of us pray aloud. Lord God I need to win the contest; with two hungry kids, overdue bills to pay at home and a no good boyfriend fucking the neighbor next door back in Chicago right now Lord. Suddenly the crowd erupts with applause and laughter. That joke brought the house down. Mary finishes her routine and meets with Rodney and James and says; how did I do.

They Look deep into her eyes and say; don't

ever do that to us again. You almost gave both of us a heart attack!

The last team finished and all teams are called back to the stage to receive the winning scores. Master of ceremony says third place goes to the team from Nebraska. First and second place is between team Wisconsin and Chicago three broke comics. Drum beat please; and the first place winner is team Wisconsin!

All top three winners will move on to the finals in New York City at the historic Apollo Theater in one month. The team is grateful for second place and gives thanks.

Mary and Tim go on to their date. Tim is familiar with the Saint Louis scene, especially the downtown Saint Louis night life. He selects a small well known family restaurant that serves late night meals, chicken and waffles.

They are seated and they make their orders. Tim explains his life story and he's from the Deep South. Mary explains her life to Tim, to a certain point not telling all. Tim says he wants to be able to know more about her and her about him.

Their dinner arrives with the smell of a mother's kitchen. Hot chicken wings and waffles. After a great dinner they take a walk in the park, next to the river walk that over looks the Mississippi River, looking at the boats pass by with their lights on. A romantic setting with a full moon this night.

Tim says I won the bet of the team moving on to New York. Now I have to take my winning by kissing you on the cheek. Mary says I don't remember that being the prize, just dinner. A kiss on the cheek you say, Tim says yes. Mary says I think I can make this one exception.

Tim leans over to her. They look deeply into each other's eyes and Tim takes his kiss on her cheek. They continue walking hand and hand down the river walk. They see a horse draw carriage and hire the horseman to carry Mary back to her hotel, as they settle in for the night. They the team all later the next day returns to the windy city.

With the winds blowing off of Lake Michigan; James finds and buys a better used truck and takes his family out on the town for food, fun and games. Mary buys a white colored family van and takes her family shopping.

Rodney is working the phone for sponsorship and investing in three broke comics branding. Later that night he is having dinner with his girl friend and future wife to be Traci.

Rodney and Traci arrive at one of Chicago finest restaurant in the downtown area.

After being seated they both discuss their plans for the future. A loving couple; holding each other's hands and making sweet small talk, as to the rest of their evening plans.

Rodney is explaining to Traci of his team success and the upcoming trip to New York City for the finals.

Traci adds her input and thoughts to the situation. Honey she says; don't you need a real job. With your master degree a lot of firms will hire you. These two other team members are people you're parading around the country with, are so beneath you. Aren't these people from the lower parts of town?

You forgot about our weekend in one month, with my parents at their new beach home on the Lake Michigan shores. I think father wants to offer you a job at his business. He knows you're not working at this time.

Rodney maintains his composure and says, "I am working as a comedian and have a talent for making people laugh and I'm learning the business side of entertainment. I'm hoping you can see it from my point of view."

Traci responses, yes dear follow your dream and when you wake up from your dream you're going to need a real 9 to 5 job. Give me the things I need in life, like a big house and trips to Europe, I'm just saying.

Rodney says just for tonight, let's just agree to disagree. Finish our dinner and retire for the night. They both agree.

Mary the next day arrives to work with the new van with Ms. Marilyn in the passenger seat as her other friend Ms. Sally, the player hater observed from just arriving at work my way of the city bus with envy.

At lunch Mary and Marilyn are laughing at their table and Sally was not asked to join them. Ms. Sally's envy is to the boiling point. At the end of the work day, Mary and Marilyn depart from the parking lot and don't even offer Sally a ride home. The envy pot is about to explode, as Sally waits at the bus stop for a ride home. Mary and Marilyn are observing her from a distance and laughing. They agree Sally has been punished enough.

They drive up slowly to the bus stop as it beings to rain and lower the passenger window and say, do you need a ride home. Sally reluctantly gets in the back seat. Mary and Marilyn can barely contain themselves with smiles on their faces looking straight ahead. There is complete silence in the van. Sally breaks the silence and says with rain water dripping from her face, "If anybody says a word or make a joke about my player hating, you both know what I carry in my bag."

"Now drive me home first." Mary says

"yes ma'am right away", as the threesome partnership is renewed. Later that evening Mary receives a phone call from her ex live in boyfriend, asking to come back into her life. She replies that issue is for another day; I'm tired and hang up the cell phone.

New York

New York City, the Big Apple. The great city that never sleeps at night. The world center of commerce, entertainment on Broadway. It's only right that it host the finals of the comedy contest. With the New York skyline as the back ground, and the historic Apollo Theater as the platform. This is the winning combination the nation and world is waiting for. So let the party begin.

A month has passed and the team leaves Chi- town and arrives at JFK airport. James brings his wife along for support and to make the trip a second honeymoon. They are taxied to the big apple with its tall building and uptown to their Harlem hotel. They can see the famous lighted sign of the Apollo Theater from their hotel rooms.

James asks to speak to Rodney in private in the hallway before the team takes a nap after the long flight.

James says what about Traci, is she coming to support you? No Rodney says. Last night she gave me back our engagement ring. Sorry about that bother.

The two men retire to their rooms for a well desired rest.

Mary lays down across her very soft king size bed. Her cell phone rings its Tim caller I. D.; she answers saying hi baby what's up.

Tim says he's working at the Apollo

Theater right now, getting the lighting just right for your big night tomorrow. Have you had dinner, do you want to go out. No she says, I'm tired from the flight. Tim says can I bring over some Chinese shrimp and fried rice later baby. Tim says what's your room number and time to come through.

Well I don't know, will you behave yourself. Tim says yes; ok. I'll text you the information baby, good bye.

The sun rises over the New York skyline. Rodney and James are having an early breakfast while the ladies sleep late. They are informed that there will be talent scouts looking for new Hollywood projects, and tonight's show will be televised.

They discuss informing Mary of this news. It is decided not to tell her, because she had just come out of new comic nerves behavior hospital.

The night of the finals contest has arrived. The crowd is flowing in. The Apollo theater mar key sign is a blaze.

With two million dollars on the line, for the

first place contest winners. Every comedian will bring their best material.

There is a meet and greet going on just for comedians, the press and talent scouts. There is even a three person comedy team from across the pond London England with one female member.

Rodney and James are working the crowd as usual. Mary goes over to introduce herself to the female within the British team with the name tag of Alice. Mary says hello and Alice immediately goes on the offence; saying. I know who you are; I'm here to destroy you and your team members!

You and your buddy's aren't going to take away first place with our monies. I will destroy you in front of these talent scouts and television.

Alice walks away from Mary with her nose in the air. This is the first time she hears that talent scouts and the television world would be watching.

The old feelings of nerves are starting to

creep back in her head. Those demons of doubt want back in her mind.

She looks at Rodney and James and explains to both of them what she encountered with Alice.

They both comfort her to build her confident. She asks them did they know about the talent scouts and television. They both jointly say with straight faces, No!

Mary does her job of drawing from the fish bowl once again. She draws the number 6 out of 15 teams. Tim her new man gives a kiss on the cheek and wishes her good luck.

Now it's time for the big show. The audience is seated. The lights are dimmed and the curtains are pulled back. The stage is ablaze with lights.

The MC comes to center stage and welcomes the audience. Then ask for 30 seconds of silence to remember the comedians that once graced this history stage.......thank you.

Master of ceremonies the rules are as follows five minutes per comic. Third place 200,000 dollars, second place 600,000 dollars, and first place two million dollars. The rest of you loser's 20,000 dollars each. So get ready to be entertained.

The bell songs and the first team take the stage, other teams follow. Now its three broke comics turn. Rodney goes first, then James, now Mary.

The British team takes to the stage and they do a good job. The last comic team finishes.

All teams are asked to return to the stage. Master of ceremonies is handed the first envelope. Three Broke Comics team is holding hands in silent prayer.

Master of ceremonies says and the third place winner is the California team. MC is handed the next envelope and says, second and first teams are tide by the score of 97 British and 97 Three Broke Comics.

By comedian rules to break the tie, there has to be a two minute face off. With one member of each team, to be selected my coin toss.

The winner of the coin toss has the right to

choose from the other team; the member that they feel is the weakest link to go up against.

Both teams move toward the MC, the British is the visiting team, so they can chose heads or tail. They choose head; MC flips the coin and it goes high in the air as if is suspended in its own atmosphere. The audience is transfixed on the coin as it falls to the floor and lands, its head.

British team huddles for a few second and says we choose Mary.

Mary and her player hater Alice will go two minutes head to head to determine the winner. No insults will be off limits.

There will be a 15 minutes intermission. Alice gives Mary the evil eye and the trigger finger as to say your ass is mind!

Mary hastily runs to the women rest room passing Rodney, James and Tim on the way. She goes into a stall and throws up her lunch.

She comes out of the stall to wash her face and there is a wash woman with a bucket and mop at work. She stands beside Mary and says I been watching you and Alice. Pay no attention to her child.

Your problem is you're too busy taking it up your ASS! Mary is shocked by the language but listens. Don't let other people define you. You're a Queen Lady; the best at whatever you put your hand too.

God did not make a mistake with you child. Your here for God's glory; from Chicago to New York; think about it.

I once was in your shoes a long time ago on that same stage. I could have been a big star. I started listening to the wrong voices of people that didn't want anything out of life; with no dreams of their own. Instead of picking me up; their goal was to bring me down to their level. My man gives me drugs, alcohol and left me with two kids to rise on my own. My time has passed; your time is now.

There a knock on the restroom door, a voice says it's time. Mary wipes the tears from her eyes, as her cell phone rings.

It's her ex-boy friend saying he wants back into her life. She says to him with confident;

get a job. Then dopes her cell phone in the water filled mop bucket.

Mary says to the wash woman, I'll buy another one; they both laugh. Mary departs from the restroom, takes a few steps away and feels she has to go back and thank the wash woman. Mary re-enters the ladies room to her surprise, the wash woman is nowhere to be found; as if she has disappeared. The only thing she found was the doo rag head ban, she was wearing on the sink.

Mary asks a stage hand, where can she find the janitor wash woman. Stage hand says there is no woman janitor working at the Apollo. The janitor is a man and he's not due in now, until an hour from now.

Mary walks down the passage way to the stage focused, with laser fixed eyes.

She meets Rodney, James and Tim as they are very concerned about her state of mind! Stops and says, "I pity the Brit."

Mary and Alice walk to center stage. MC says the two minutes start now!

Alice delivers the first insult.

Mary fires back hard.

Alice delivers both barrows.

Mary drops a bomb on Alice head.

Alice hits Mary with a straight right hand.

Mary delivers an upper cut to the jaw; that lifts Alice off the floor. Back and forth they sling mud jokes at each other at the speed of sound. The bell rings times up.

Master of ceremonies comes out to center stage and is handed the judges envelope. The crowd silence is deafening; you could hear a mouse pass gas. He says with authority, the first place winner is Three Broke Comics. The fans applauses with a tremendous standing ovation.

Alice is disappointed, but shakes Mary hand in good sportsmanship. The Three Broke Comic team is crying with joy!

A talent agent hands his business card to Rodney and says call me. The winning team also receives flowers.

As the dust of joy settles, sadness moves in. They each realize their union is over. Each one has to go, their each separate ways. Rodney the rock of the group, even has tears in his eyes, says we may not see each other every day but remember.

"We are Three Broke Comics forever"

The End

Coming Soon

The Re-Mix
The Comedy
By
Al Katar

Credits/Contributors

Education News Network (ENN)

Of Pensacola, Florida

Mr. Cedric (Cid) Langham

ENN Vice President Chicago, Illinois

Publicist

Patricia Ann Pryor

Country Line Music.Com

Song "My Heart" written by AL Pryor

Three Broke Comics.Com

Writing Staff

Scratch Kids Products

Bug Tubes

Spencer For Hire Graphics of Pensacola, Florida, for front and back cover.

Avonbuynow.com

Al Katar was born a baby of the Civil Rights Movement in the mid 1950's. A child of the 60's. A man of the 70's and a storyteller of the 21st century, who hasn't forgotten the great writers of the past. He writes in the action, suspense, drama, comedy and the everyday "just be real with me story" genre. From stories titled "The Last Warrior", "Gator Restaurant", "Third Strike", "Drop Off Zone", "The Monkey", "Pensacola Sharks", "Meet Black People" just to name a few and also a bonus feature "Education, The Sitcom", Katar consider himself to be a transfer writer.

Katar to his knowledge is the only writer to publish a three book trilogy on the black pirate "Captain Scratch". He is looking for representation in the film, book and entertainment industry. Katar hopes to build a meaningful relationship and partner with progressive Hollywood studios to maximize sales of a number of his books to be made into movies. He believes with the right management team and investment network the sky is the limit. Some wise person once said only when a writer is stretched and has suffered, that writer will become better. Katar is ready and willing to suffer and to be stretched all the more. See Amazon/Al katar/Books.

Apparel

At

Three Broke Comics.Com

Franchise Opportunities

At

Three Broke Comics franchise
opportunities information available
at www.threebrokecomics.com

Made in the USA
Middletown, DE
05 February 2021